Delhi Visit

Ann Morris

Photographs by Heidi Larson

A&C Black · London

Kirin and Poonam were getting ready to visit their mum's family in Delhi, over the winter holidays. They had been to Delhi the year before, and Kirin was looking forward to seeing her cousin Rajiv again.

The two sisters lived in London with their mum and dad. In Delhi, they would be staying in a big house with Mum's brothers and their families.

Kirin and Poonam were going to share a room. They would be able to stay up late and talk, as long as Mum didn't hear them.

3

That night, Dad took
out some of the
photographs from
their last trip to
Delhi.

'Remember when we
went to see the film
with Sri Devi?' said
Poonam. 'She's a
great dancer.'

'I do remember. You
kept practising all
those dances when we
got home,' said Kirin.

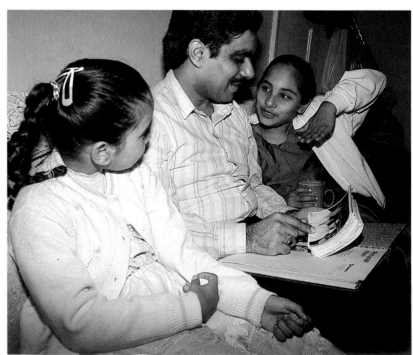

Dad wasn't going to Delhi this time because
he had to stay and look after his bookshop in
London. He sold books from India to people
who could read languages such as Hindi,
Urdu and Punjabi. He was teaching Kirin
and Poonam to read some Hindi.

Sometimes, Dad sold pictures from India of
Hindu gods and goddesses. If there was a
specially beautiful one, he might keep it for
the family shrine at home.

5

Mum wanted to buy some presents to take to Delhi, so the next morning they set off for the market.

On the way, they stopped at the temple to make an offering of prayers and money.

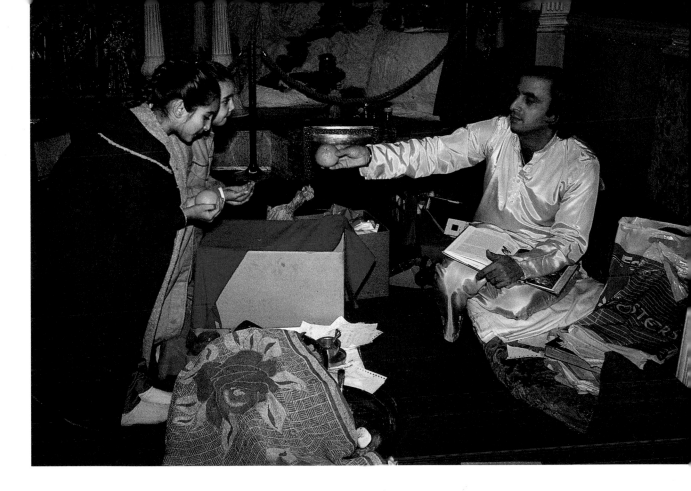

The temple priest gave them prasad – food which had been blessed. That day, the prasad was an orange.

In the market, Kirin found just the right present for Rajiv, a set of coloured pencils. 'I know he likes drawing,' she said. 'Remember that picture of an aeroplane he gave me?'

7

'What about some sweets for Veenu?' said Poonam, holding up her favourites.

Kirin bought a Walkman for her cousin Ramesh. She was sure he'd like that. He was always listening to Michael Jackson instead of doing his homework.

'Do you think they have computers
at their school?' she asked.

Mum bought track
suits for their cousins
and a salwar chemise
for each of the girls.

They picked out new
shoes as well.

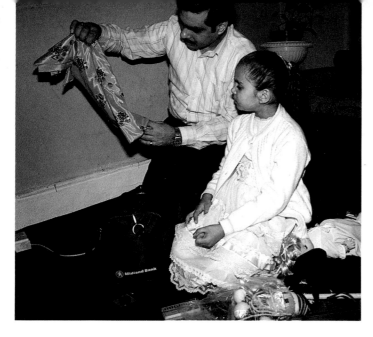

Dad helped them to pack their suitcases. 'Give Aunty Rita my love,' he said. 'I hope she likes this material.'

'There won't be enough room for the dolls,' said Poonam. 'Never mind,' said Kirin. 'I'm going to carry mine on the 'plane.'

Grandma gave them a big hug goodbye. She and Grandpa would be staying with Dad while Kirin and Poonam were away.

Dad drove them to the airport. They had a cold drink and watched the big TV screens for their flight number to come up.

'Be good!' said Dad, as he waved them off. For just a moment, Kirin wasn't sure she really wanted to go. But once she was on the 'plane, she started thinking about all the nice things she would do in Delhi.

It was a long flight, more than seven hours. When Uncle Arvind came to pick them up at the airport, Kirin and Poonam could hardly stay awake.

All the way to the house, Mum kept asking about the places they could see out of the window. She wanted to know about the new shops on Janpeth and a hundred other things.

Aunty Rita was pleased to see them. Poonam
and Kirin gave her the material from Dad.
They remembered that Aunty Rita was
always sewing. She had made some curtains
for their room and now she was working on a
new suit for a wedding.

Then they went out on to the balcony for a
look at the street. Down below was a scooter
rickshaw and a man on a bicycle. 'Now I
really feel as if I'm here,' said Poonam.

Mum helped them to unpack their bags and
put their dolls to bed. 'They'll need a good
rest after such a long trip,' said Kirin. The
two girls also had a nap.

14

After a long sleep and a cool shower, Kirin and Poonam went up to the roof, where Aunty Rita and Mum and Aunty Tara were having some tea.

There were biscuits and snacks, and cold drinks of 'Thums-Up' for the girls.
'I remember you liked that last year,' said Aunty Tara.

'Now, what would you like to do?' asked Mum. 'Rajiv is coming to see you later. Why don't you phone Veenu and ask if she would like to go and see a film?'

Poonam wanted to see
'Shahansha', the latest film
with Amitabh Bhachan.
'Let's go soon,' she said. 'It
won't come to London for
ages. Even Renu hasn't seen
it, and her dad gets all the videos.'

When they had finished their drinks, Aunty Kamala listened to them read. It made Kirin think about all the book times with Dad in London.

'We wanted Dad to come with us, but he had to stay at home and work,' Kirin explained.

'Maybe Dad will come next time,' said Aunty Kamala, who understood how she felt.

It was lovely and warm on the roof. Mum said that the laundry would dry in no time, even though it was the middle of winter.

In summer, it was too hot to sit on the roof but, in winter, the Aunties liked to do their sewing and chat up there, or on the cool, shady balcony below.

It seemed a little strange to be so far away from England, but there was one thing which was almost the same as home. The family shrine had a statue of Ganesh, just like the one in their house in London.

That afternoon, Rajiv did come over to see them. He gave Poonam a ride on his new bike, and he wanted to hear all about the friends he'd met when he had stayed with them in England.

'When you get back, tell Garry I'm in the football team at school now,' he said.

Later on, Aunty Gita needed to go to the market, so they walked down to the main road to hire a rickshaw.

On the way, they tried to read all the advertisements. 'You'll have to practise your Hindi,' said Aunty Gita. 'Then you'll be able to help your dad when you get home.'

22

When they reached the market, they jumped down and Poonam paid the driver five rupees for the ride. 'Now stay close to me,' said Aunty Gita.

They stopped at the dry-cleaners first, and then Aunty Gita went to collect her new sari from the tailor.

'I wish we'd been here for Diwali,' said Poonam. 'We could have sent Dad a really good card. Let's send him one of these instead.'

That night, they called Dad on the telephone.
They told him all about how Aunty Rita had
liked her present, about tea on the roof and
'Thums-Up' and about the bike ride and the
room they shared. And of course, about the film
they were going to see with Amitabh Bhachan.

25